Barney the Bear Killer
Book 1

The Grizzly

Barney the Bear Killer
Book 1

The Grizzly

By

Pat L. Sargent

Illustrated by
Jane Lenoir

Ozark Publishing, Inc.
P.O. Box 228
Prairie Grove, AR 72753

Library of Congress cataloging-in-publication data

Sargent, Pat, 1936-
The grizzly / Pat Sargent ; illustrated by Jane
Lenoir.
p. cm. — (Barney the bear killer ; 1)
Summary: An abandoned puppy finds a home
with a farm family and earns the name Barney the
Bear Killer.
ISBN 1-56763-054-5. (cloth : alk. paper). —
ISBN 1-56763-055-3
(paper : alk. paper)
1. Dogs—Juvenile fiction. [1. Dogs—Fiction.
2. Farm life—Fiction.] I. Lenoir, Jane, 1950- ill. II.
Title. III. Series.
PZ10.3.S244Gr 1996
[Fic]—dc20

96-33906
CIP
AC

Ozark Publishing, Inc.
P.O. Box 228
Prairie Grove, AR 72753
Ph: 1-800-321-5671

Printed in the United States of America

Inspired by

the many times my dad took me coon hunting with him and his cousin, Ed. Ed had black-and-tan coonhounds, and the smartest, bravest one of all was ole Barney. As we waited on cold, moonlit nights, Barney would be the first to pick up a trail. When he let out his bay, Ed would say, "That's ole Barney! Listen to him, Pat, he's got a silver tongue."

Dedicated to

my dad, Herschel P. Shull, a teacher of forty-eight years. Dad taught me many things. He taught me to love and respect animals. But the thing I remember most, is that, when we would go hunting, he'd say, "Now, we won't kill more than we can eat. We'll kill only what we need for food. Always remember that, Pat." Even though you're gone now, I think of you often. I still love you, Daddy. And to my dear husband, Dave, who encouraged me to write.

Foreword

When Barney is accused of killing a newborn baby calf, it hurts him very much. Bossy, the baby calf's mother, tells Barney that a huge brown bear killed her baby. Barney knows that in order to clear his good name and to protect the only place he's ever loved, he must find the killer bear before it strikes again. Barney earns the reputation of being the guardian of Farmer John's place.

Contents

Barney the Bear Killer
Book 1

The Grizzly

Chapter One

Scared and Alone

The little coonhound was only twelve weeks old when the car he was riding in pulled over and stopped on the lonely country road. A tall gruff man jumped out from under the wheel and jerked open the back door. He glared at the skinny little pup that was lying in the floorboard of the car. Then, as though his heart were made of stone, he reached in and grabbed the pup by the nape of the neck and

1

jerked him out the door. He tossed him to the side of the road and said, "There, you mangy little hound! Find yourself a new home, one that wants you, 'cause I sure don't! I've got too many mouths to feed now!" And with those not-so-kind words of farewell, he jumped into his car and took off.

The young puppy stood there shaking, partly because of the cold, freezing rain and partly because he was getting weak from hunger. The little pup hardly ever got anything to eat—only a few table scraps that were tossed out the back door when one of the kids felt sorry for him. And that didn't happen but once or twice each week.

He looked to the east, then looked to the west, wondering which way he should go. Then, cold and hungry and looking for shelter from the driving rain, he turned in the direction the sun should be and trotted slowly down the road.

Early the next morning, just before dawn—just when he was about to give up hope--a wonderful smell tickled his nose. He didn't know it at the time, but it was the smell of ham and bacon smoking. And it was coming from Farmer John's place.

Farmer John had butchered two pigs the day before, and the bacon and hams were hanging from the rafters of a small wooden shed that stood out behind the house. Farmer John smoked meats in it, and so, the small shed was called a smokehouse.

The little dog, with his nose in the air, followed the smell. When he finally came to the smokehouse, he nosed his way around it, trying to find a way to get inside. Finally, he located a hole in the wall, on the back side, down close to the ground. The hole was too small to crawl through, so he started gnawing away at the half-rotten wooden boards.

Inside the warm, cozy house, Farmer John sat at the table, listening to the weather report. He was on his last cup of coffee.

He pulled on his coat, then headed for the smokehouse to check the hickory chips that were burning in the big iron kettle under the meat. He didn't want the fire to go out. They were almost out of meat, and they would need the bacon and hams to make it through the winter.

When he raised the latch on the door and stepped inside, he stopped. The small table that held the spices and salt had been turned over, and everything was lying on the ground.

"What in tarnation?" he yelled. "A varmint's been in here!"

The yell woke the little pup. He crouched behind the pan of hickory chips that were soaking in water—too scared to move or cry out.

Farmer John's keen eyes made a quick search of the ground under the hanging meat, looking for tracks or some kind of sign.

The dirt floor was hard and packed, and he found only parts of a track here and there. Thinking that it had been a fox, or a bobcat, maybe, he turned and ran out in such a hurry that he neglected to close and bolt the door.

"A shot of rock salt will fix that pesky varmint!" he said, as he ran to the house for his gun.

Now, the frightened pup didn't really understand what Farmer John had said, but he had understood his tone of voice. And he wasted no time in crossing the floor and climbing over the twelve-inch board that was nailed across the bottom of the doorway. As fast as his tired little legs would carry him, he ran for the safety of the woods.

Farmer John ran out with his shotgun, loading it as he ran, yelling, "Okay, you pesky little varmint! Come and get it! I'm ready for you now!"

In the smokehouse, nothing moved—nothing except a few wisps of smoke that drifted up toward the high rafters.

Farmer John leaned his gun against the wall, scratched his head, and said, "Well now, if this don't beat all. How in tarnation did something get in here in the first place?"

He began a search, and it wasn't long until he discovered the hole the pup had crawled through. It was down low, near the center of the back wall, behind the pan of hickory chips.

He shook his head and said, "I've been meaning to fix that hole. I should have replaced those rotten boards last summer."

He went inside and scooted the pan of hickory chips over to the hole in the wall. He worked until the pan completely covered the hole. Then he went back into the house, took off his coat, and pulled on his insulated coveralls. He headed down the lane to get the cows, muttering, "Because of that pesky varmint, I'll be milking later than usual this morning. Just when I promised the girls we'd find a Christmas tree today."

The rain finally stopped, and the hungry pup lay in the edge of the woods watching everything that went on that day. He watched as the cows were driven into the corral, into the barn, and out again—not really understanding what any of it meant. And the hardest part of all to figure out, was, that evening, it was all done again!

The temperature dropped even lower when darkness came creeping over the farm. When Farmer John checked the outdoor thermometer on the outside wall of the barn, he shook his head, and said, "Burr-rrr-rr! It's down to twenty-five! She's gonna get cold tonight!"

Farmer John hurried to the house and the waiting fire that was burning in the big open fireplace.

Later that evening, hunger got the best of the little pup and he went back to the small hole in the smoke-house wall. Something was wrong! It was covered up! Now what? If he didn't find food and a warm place to sleep, come morning, he'd be dead.

Chapter Two

The Unwanted Visitor

When Farmer John passed the smokehouse, he glanced toward it, his eyes searching for signs of the intruder. At first, he noticed nothing unusual. Then suddenly, he stopped dead in his tracks. There, on the back side of the smokehouse, lying on the ground, was a small varmint.

Farmer John moved closer. It was dark, so it was hard to tell just what it was.

Farmer John hurried to the house, eased open the back door, crossed the room, and reached up over the mantle for his gun. He took it down, slipped in two shells, pulled back the hammer, and said, "Now, by doggies! I'm gonna get the pesky little varmint that's been into my smokehouse trying to get my smoked bacon and hams!"

He hurried out the door and eased around the corner of the smokehouse. And sure enough, there, lying on the ground, was the pesky little varmint!

Standing there in the darkness, Farmer John squinted his eyes. He took off his hat, scratched his head, and said, "Looks to me like it's dead. Must have frozen to death!"

With his gun, he poked the small varmint. When it didn't move, he poked it again. There was no movement at all. Nothing.

Knowing for sure that it wasn't a skunk, Farmer John leaned his gun against the smokehouse wall, then knelt down.

Slowly, a smile crept over his face. He reached up and tipped back his hat and said, "Would you look at this! It's a black and tan! Now where in blue blazes did this little coonhound come from?"

He hurriedly examined the pup. He saw that it was a male, but he didn't know if it was alive or dead. He placed his big hand over its small heart. There was no heartbeat. He felt again—this time, holding his breath. At first, he wasn't sure. He couldn't be certain, but, wait! There it was—a small but steady thump, thump, thump. He reached down and very gently picked up the pup and carried it into the house.

Molly was in the kitchen. She had just taken a blackberry cobbler out of the oven. She said, without turning around, "Supper's almost ready, John. Maybe you'd like to warm up by the fire before we eat."

Farmer John stopped behind Molly and said, "Look at this, Molly. Look what I found."

Molly turned around. She gave a happy shriek when she saw the pup. Then she noticed his ribs showing through his skinny little sides. She saw his tired little face, his dry nose, and his red, swollen feet. She also saw that he wasn't moving.

Molly said, "Oh, John, that poor little thing's dead! Why did you bring a dead dog into the house? What in the world's gotten into you?"

"Easy, Molly," Farmer John said. "He's not dead. I felt a slight heartbeat. Get something to lay him on. We'll put him over by the fire. He's almost froze to death!"

Molly ran to the linen closet and grabbed an old blanket. She hurried over to the fireplace and, turning it, warmed it on both sides. She laid it on one side of the hearth and said, "Hurry, John, put him here . . . careful now . . . not too close to the fire."

With tears in her eyes, Molly watched as Farmer John gently laid the pup on the blanket.

"You can tell just by looking at him that he's had nothing to eat," she said. "This little thing's been starved to death. It's cruel—inhumane—to do an animal this way! Who would do such a thing?"

Farmer John worked with the pup for a good five minutes; then he stopped, looked up, and shook his head.

As he slowly got to his feet, Molly caught her breath. "Oh, John, no! Please don't tell me he's dead!"

Farmer John didn't answer. He didn't say a word. He just stood there.

Molly ran out of the room. She hurried to their bedroom and grabbed a small hand mirror off the dresser. She rushed back to the living room, handed it to Farmer John, and said, "Here, John, check him like you check baby calves."

Farmer John took the mirror, then handed it back to Molly and said, "You hold it. I'll try massaging his heart and chest. It might help stimulate his circulation."

Molly held the mirror in front of the little coonhound's nose. And as they knelt beside him, Farmer John gave it his best. He massaged his heart, then rubbed his sides, and rubbed his legs, and rubbed his swollen little feet.

Finally, after what seemed like an eternity, Molly said, "It's no use, John. He's dead."

With tears on her cheeks, Molly stood up, smoothed her dress, and straightened a strand of hair that had fallen across her face.

"You're a mite hasty, aren't you, Molly? Look at this!" For the first time, Farmer John's voice sounded chipper.

Molly dropped to her knees and stared in disbelief. A very tiny cloudy spot was forming on the mirror. They both smiled, for they knew then that the pup was alive.

Farmer John took one end of the blanket and pulled it up over the pup. He looked at Molly's worried face and said, "Don't worry. He'll be all right. You'd better get something warm for him to eat. A little bowl of gravy will do just fine."

Well, by the time they had fed the little dog, and he had warmed up by the fire, he was feeling a great deal better. He sat up and looked around, wondering where he was—thankful for the warm fire and the satisfied feeling in his stomach.

It was at that moment that Farmer John and Molly's little girls, Amber, April, and Ashley, jumped up off their bedroom floor and turned off their radio. They hurried to the kitchen. Their job, every night, was to set the table.

As they entered the den, they stopped and stared. For there, lying on the hearth, was the cutest little hound dog they had ever seen. They were used to being around animals, so they knew better than to make any noise or sudden moves that might frighten him. They eased over to where he was lying.

Molly looked up and smiled. Then, Farmer John asked, "Think this little hound would make a good Christmas present?"

With glowing faces, they asked, "May we keep him, Daddy? Really?"

"Yep, I reckon you can keep him," Farmer John answered. "I've been needing a good hunting dog."

About that time, two-year-old Ashley began shaking her head. All eyes turned toward her.

Molly asked, "What is it, honey? What's wrong?"

"I don't want that dumb ole dog, Mama!" Ashley said.

They held their breath. They were shocked that she did not want the pup. They tried to agree on things that affected the family. They even voted when they had to. So, no matter if Ashley was the youngest, if she didn't want the dog, they would have to vote.

Molly reached up and, stroking the little girl's hair, asked, "But, why, honey? Why don't you want the puppy? It's a pretty little dog."

Ashley's big brown eyes were brimming over as she said, "Because its ears are too long!"

Everyone tried to hide their smiles. They were relieved. They could work around this problem.

Amber said, "Maybe by the time he's grown, his ears won't look so long. The rest of him will grow, too, you know."

Ashley looked at Amber with a puzzled look on her face. Then, just as suddenly as she had objected to the long-eared pup, she accepted him. She leaned down and planted a big wet kiss on his tired little face!

"Well! I reckon that settles it!" Farmer John said, as he gave the dog a pat and got to his feet.

Molly stood up and said, "Run wash your hands, it's time to eat."

The girls washed their hands, then ran and set the table. All the excitement had given them a big appetite!

That night at the dinner table, they were a bit noisier than usual. When Farmer John finished eating, he stood up, pushed his chair under the table, and said, "Since tomorrow is Saturday, I guess we'd better find us a Christmas tree. We'll need one to put your present under." The girls giggled and looked over at the pup, who was sprawled out on the blanket.

When the little dog heard the giggling, he opened one eye and gazed at the girls. And for the very first time in his life, he felt happiness

and contentment. As he fell into a
deep sleep, he was thinking, "Yep,
I'm gonna like this place."

Chapter Three

The Christmas Puppy

The next morning, Farmer John hurried through his morning chores. In the house, Molly got the girls up and dressed. They were excited, for today was the day they'd been waiting for—the day to find a Christmas tree.

When they finished eating, they jumped up and cleared the table. It was a longtime tradition that all the members of the family go along when it was time to cut the tree, for locating just the right one was a big job. And it was usually the girls who made the final decision.

Farmer John zipped Ashley's snowsuit, and said, as he tied her hat, "There you go, June Bug. You're all set!" She hurried out the door right behind Amber and April.

"June Bug" was Ashley's pet name. Farmer John had given all three girls a nickname. Ashley was "June Bug," Amber was "Nicki," and April was "J.J.," which stood for "Jabber Jaws." He even had a pet name for Molly. When he wanted to tease her, he called her "Squiggs."

When Farmer John walked out the back door, he looked around for the pup. It was lying on the edge of the porch, watching everyone.

Molly, too, saw the pup. She asked, "What are we going to call him, John? He needs a name."

Farmer John took off his hat and scratched his head, then replied, "I've been thinking about that. I had a dog when I was a boy. His name was Barney."

Molly smiled and said, "Why, that's a nice name. Let's call him Barney."

A sad look came over Farmer John's face. He said, as he shook his head, "That cur lying over there could never measure up to my Barney."

Molly stiffened. She said, "He's not a cur, John! A cur is a mongrel. And a mongrel is a dog of mixed breed. This pup is a true-bred black and tan. You can tell by looking at him that he's special!"

Right away, it was evident to Farmer John that Molly liked the new pup. She wasn't usually that touchy. He slapped his leg with the palm of his hand, gave a sharp whistle, and said, "Here, dog!"

The frail little pup got up and walked across the porch. It stopped at Farmer John's feet, raised its head, and looked him in the eye.

"Well, at least he's got spunk!" Farmer John said, with a chuckle.

Molly and the girls climbed into the small trailer that Farmer John had fastened to the back of the tractor. It took a lot of coaxing to get the pup to stay in the trailer. When he finally settled into one spot, they took off for the woods.

It took a good hour to find the perfect tree. It was just right! It was exactly the right height and exactly the right width. And it had just the right look. No doubt about it, it was perfect!

They placed the tree in the trailer, then everyone climbed in. This time, the pup tried to jump in, but he fell short. He tried two more times without any luck. He was too short in the poop!

Farmer John stood watching, thinking, "Yep! He's a fighter!" He reached down and picked up the pup and tossed him in the trailer.

The pup trotted to the front, sniffed the top of the tree, then curled up beside it.

They spent the rest of the day decorating the tree. Molly popped a big pan of popcorn, and Amber and April, using a needle and a thread, made strings of popcorn for the tree. They also strung cranberries. Then, they alternated three strands, using popcorn, then cranberries, popcorn, cranberries, popcorn, cranberries. The tree was very colorful with the red garlands and the white garlands and the red-and-white garlands.

The pup sat on the hearth, watching Molly and the little girls with a great deal of interest. This was something new. Since this was his first Christmas, he had never seen a Christmas tree.

That night after milking, when Farmer John walked in and saw the tree, he knew that it had been well worth their efforts. He took off his hat, held it over his heart, and said, "Ladies, that tree is a work of art!"

As he pulled off his boots and his insulated coveralls, he couldn't help but notice their proud smiles. He washed his hands and combed his hair. Tonight was special!

After they had finished eating, Farmer John went into the living room and sat down in his favorite chair. As he leaned it back, the pup got up and crossed over to him. It lay down at his feet. It looked up at Farmer John with big trusting eyes.

44

Well, it's hard for anyone to resist a look like that. Farmer John hadn't had a dog since his old Barney died. He hadn't even wanted one. He reached down and gave the little pup a gentle slap on the side. And right then and there, a special bond was established. Molly smiled when she saw the warm look pass between them.

And that was how the little pup happened to stay in the house all night for the first time. Farmer John had made him a nice bed in the barn, but they fell into a deep sleep, and they slept there all night long. The little pup didn't sleep in the cold barn, and Farmer John didn't sleep in his bed.

When Farmer John woke up the next morning, he looked down at the sleeping pup and thought, "Would you look at that. The little scoundrel stayed by my side all night—just like ole Barney used to."

After two hot cups of coffee, Farmer John headed to the barn to prepare for the morning milking. Halfway down the lane, he felt eyes watching him. He stopped and looked back. The pup was standing inside the gate, looking at him with those big eyes.

"Okay, come on. You can go, but you're still a little too young to work the cows. Now, my ole Barney was a border collie. Let me tell you, that was one smart cow dog! He knew what to do without me having to say a word."

As the pup ambled over to where he was waiting, Farmer John thought, "At least he's game."

The last cow was leaving the barn when a terrible commotion broke out near the chicken house. Molly ran out of the house, and Farmer John ran out of the barn. They stood and stared at the scene.

The pup had a raccoon by the tail and was sitting back on all four feet! They went round and round, and the raw egg the young raccoon had in its mouth fell to the ground with a splat!

The raccoon twisted around and grabbed the pup by the nose. The pup yelped and let go.

When the raccoon felt the pup turn loose of its tail, it took off across the field as fast as its legs could go!

The pup "gave tongue," or let out a bay, for the first time, and he was right on the raccoon's tail!

Farmer John said, "Listen to him, Molly! Listen to that! Did you ever hear anything so pretty? That dog's got a silver tongue!" Then, "Go git him, Barney! You teach him to stay out of the chicken house! I'm tired of losing eggs to that rascal!"

Molly thought, "He's so excited, he forgot and called him Barney."

So nothing more was said about what to name the little pup, because he had pretty much proven himself to

Farmer John. The fact that he could keep that pesky little Roy Raccoon out of the chicken house was a good start. And so, from that time on, the pup was called Barney.

The next two weeks were spent making homemade presents, for the most part, and cookies and candies. And, of course, the traditional fruit cake. The little girls loved to help wrap the presents, and even though they promised not to tell, they knew by Christmas Eve what they were getting. Barney loved the festive mood of that first Christmas.

The next year seemed to go by fast. The days were full of exciting adventures. Barney grew strong and healthy. He was happy with his new family. He had never known such peace and love.

Chapter Four

Ole Satan

One morning in early March, Barney trotted through the woods, heading back toward the barn. He had been on his morning rabbit hunt. Chrissy Cottontail had given him the slip again. He couldn't understand how a little rabbit could run so fast!

When he crossed the lane, he heard giggling. He knew that the girls were not supposed to play this far from the house. Ole Satan was in this pasture, and they were never, never to go near Satan. Many times, Farmer John had said, "A Jersey bull is the meanest bull in the world! Don't ever turn your back on one, Barney!"

A chill ran through Barney. His eyes searched the pasture. Where was Satan?

When the two little girls reached the barbed wire fence, they looked across the field for ole Satan. When they didn't see him, they figured their daddy had moved the bull to a different pasture.

Well, Satan hadn't been moved. He was lying in the edge of the woods under a big white-oak tree. He was dozing, chewing his cud. When he heard the girls laughing, he stopped chewing and raised his head. He opened his eyes and scanned the pasture. Finally, he saw them. They were on his side of the fence!

He got to his feet. He stretched, then shook himself. The layers of muscle on his body rippled, moving like waves on an ocean. He snorted and a rumbling noise came from deep within his chest.

The girls were laughing and playing and didn't hear ole Satan's low rumble. They didn't see him coming across the pasture with his head down low—and his dark eyes beginning to blaze.

Satan's eyes were on the girls. "What are they doing in my field?" he wondered angrily. "This field is mine! They don't belong here!"

The closer he got, the madder he got. "I'll teach those little girls not to play in my field," he thought, as his massive body picked up speed.

Amber and April felt the ground begin to tremble, and then they heard a rumbling noise that sounded like far-off thunder.

Amber had been a bit uneasy ever since they had crawled under the fence. She grabbed April by the hand and said, "Come on, April, let's go. We're not supposed to be playing in this field. If Daddy sees us, he'll get mad. Let's hurry. It's going to rain. I hear thunder."

It wasn't thunder the girls heard! Satan's massive body had picked up speed, and he was coming across the field like a tornado!

When Amber looked over her shoulder and saw the huge bull, she screamed, "Run, April! Run! It's ole Satan!"

Barney had heard the rumbling noise, and he had felt the ground trembling. And then—the scream! His eyes locked in on a horrible scene. The little girls were in terrible trouble!

Ole Satan was closing in! He was frothing at the mouth. His head was down close to the ground, and a cloud of smoke was coming from his nostrils. The points of his horns were glistening in the morning sun.

The little girls were so scared. They were running as fast as their legs would carry them. They had almost reached the fence and safety, when April stumbled and fell. Amber grabbed the back of her shirt and half-drug her until they reached the fence.

Amber knew that they didn't have time to crawl through the fence, for she could feel Satan's hot breath on her neck. She did the only thing she could think of. She grabbed the bottom wire and jerked up, then shoved April under it.

It was at that exact moment, when she thought she was done for, that ole Barney lunged. He sailed through the air, and landed right on Satan's head!

Satan let out an angry bellow that could be heard for three or four miles. He slung his head from side to side, trying to sling Barney off.

Barney had Satan by the nose, but he was losing his grip. His eyes searched frantically for Amber to see if she had made it safely through the fence. He knew that he couldn't hold on much longer.

When Amber got one leg and most of her body through the fence, she let go of the wire. But she let go too soon. A rusty barb caught her in the other leg, just above the knee. The barb ripped her leg wide open! The gash was six inches long and went clear to the bone, and blood spurted as she grabbed April's hand and ran for the house.

When Barney saw that Amber was safely on the other side of the fence, he loosened his grip on Satan's nose.

When ole Satan felt Barney let go, he angrily tossed his head. His long, pointed horns caught Barney, sending him sailing high into the air.

When Barney hit the ground, he bounced and tumbled and rolled and twisted—trying to stay out from under Satan's feet.

Satan was one mad bull! He bellowed and snorted! He stomped and pawed the ground!

Finally, Barney got away from

Satan and made a nose dive for the fence. He crawled under it so fast, his stomach hardly touched the ground. He made a beeline for the house. When he reached the back gate, he sailed up and over, just as the girls were going through it. He whirled around to see if Satan was behind them.

When he saw that the bull was still inside the pasture, he breathed a sigh of relief. He had tangled with Satan before. He was a mean bull!

And back in the pasture, Satan's massive chest strained against the fence. He bellowed and pawed the ground, and in bull talk, roared, "This pasture is mine! Stay out!"

At that moment, Amber fell to the ground. Barney wondered, "Did the bull gore her?" He tried to get her to stand up. When she couldn't, he ran to the back door and began scratching the door frantically.

Molly had just turned off the radio. She'd been listening to the weather report. When she heard the scratching, she hesitated for a brief moment, then asked herself, "Now who in the world could that be?" None of the neighbors ever knocked. They usually just pushed open the door and hollered, "Hey, Molly!" or "John! You home?"

The scratching grew louder, more frantic! Molly reached up and straightened her hair, then went to the door. When she opened it and saw Barney, she knew something was wrong. His face was twisted, his mouth was tense, and his eyes were full of fear, excitement, and anger.

Molly looked past Barney and saw the girls by the gate. Amber was half-sitting, half-lying on the ground, and April was kneeling beside her.

At the sight of the girls, Molly's heart almost stopped beating. She flew down the steps and across the yard.

Amber's leg was throbbing with pain. She stared at the blood on her leg and, for a second, thought she was going to faint. Then, she gritted her teeth and clinched her fist— determined to be brave.

After first examining the long jagged gash in Amber's leg, Molly quickly checked April. She was relieved to see that April wasn't hurt.

Barney was anxious to help, but he didn't know what to do. He knew that the bleeding had to be stopped or Amber would soon bleed to death. His eyes searched Molly's face as he thought, "Oh, please hurry, Molly! Quick! Do something!"

With every passing moment, Amber grew weaker. At first, she felt sleepy. Then, she slowly drifted off into unconsciousness.

Molly carefully put her right arm under Amber's shoulders and her left arm under her legs. She gently lifted her up.

Because Molly was so scared, Amber felt light to her as she hurried the short distance to the back porch.

It had been only seconds since Molly had reached the girls. Barney felt better now that something was being done to help Amber. He didn't want her to die. He loved her. He kept thinking, "Hang on, Amber. You're gonna be all right," then, "Where's Farmer John?"

Molly laid Amber on the back porch, then ran to the small utility building where the mower, kerosene, and such things were kept. She grabbed the can of kerosene and some clean rags and hurried back to the porch.

After placing the rags under and around Amber's leg, Molly poured the open wound full of kerosene.

She knew it would burn, but she also knew that it would kill the germs the rusty barbed wire had left in the wound.

Amber didn't feel a thing. She didn't move. She didn't cry out. She was unconscious—dead to the sting, the terrible burn of the kerosene. Her face was pale, and her lips were blue.

Now that the initial shock was over, Molly knew she had to act fast. As she ran into the house, she said, "Barney, you and April watch her. I'm going to get a blanket. We can't let her go into shock."

After what seemed like ages to Barney, Molly came back with the blanket. She gently covered Amber with it. Then, she and April and Barney said a silent prayer.

Barney whined a low, sad whine, then reached down and, with his long

wet tongue, licked Amber's face
again and again. Finally, she opened
her eyes.

"You're okay," he wanted to say, but instead, he just wagged his tail and whined.

Amber reached up and touched Barney's face. She said, "Thanks, Barney. You saved my life. You saved me from ole Satan."

Molly patted Amber's shoulder and said, "Barney, go see if that's John coming—sounds like his truck."

Barney jumped off the porch and took off around the house. "Yep," he thought, with a great deal of relief, "it's Farmer John, all right."

Now, when Farmer John saw the way Barney was running, he knew something must be terribly wrong. Because ole Barney never moved very fast. He hardly ever got in a hurry.

Before the truck had stopped, Barney leaped up on the door.

Farmer John jumped out of the cab, and asked, "What's up, Barney? Something wrong?"

His question was answered when Barney gave out a sharp bark and took off around the corner of the house, glancing back a couple of times to make sure Farmer John was coming.

When he rounded the corner, Barney was relieved to see Amber sitting up. He watched as Molly put something into Amber's mouth, then held a glass of water to her lips. He figured she was giving her medicine.

"Molly's a good doctor," he thought. "She fixed my foot when I got caught in that coon trap."

Now, Farmer John was not the excitable type, so he quietly surveyed the situation. He looked Amber's leg over real good, and knowing full well that the only barbed wire on the place was strung around Satan's pasture, knew what she must have done. Without even asking, he knew that Amber had been in Satan's pasture.

He grinned and said, "Well, Nicki, look's like you're going to have yourself a souvenir. Yes sireee, a souvenir from ole Satan."

Amber's eyes searched his face. And with a great deal of relief, she thought, "He doesn't look mad." She hated it when he got mad at her.

The truth was, Farmer John was so thankful that Amber had escaped Satan's wrath with only a cut on her leg, that he forgot to get mad.

Tears came to Amber's eyes as she lowered her head and said, "I'm sorry, Daddy. I'm sorry I went into Satan's pasture. I won't do it again, Daddy. I promise."

And Farmer John knew as he gently picked her up that that was a promise she would keep. He said, "Come on, Molly. You'd better get June Bug. We need to get this girl fixed up. We'll run into town and let Doc Miller take a look at her leg."

Amber knew what that meant, but she didn't say a word. She knew that she would have to have stitches, but she was not about to complain. After all, wasn't it her own fault for doing what she'd been warned not to do?

Farmer John put Amber in the truck on her mother's lap, then April and Ashley climbed in. When he jumped in and started turning the truck around, ole Barney ran in front of the truck and came to a screeching halt.

Farmer John stuck his head out the window. He yelled, "That's a good way to get run over, Barney! What's wrong with you?"

Barney's ears were perked up, and he looked at Farmer John as if he were asking, "Can I go, too?"

Molly laughed and said, "Let him go with us. After all, he was the one who saved Amber from Satan. He wants to go along to make sure she's going to be okay."

Farmer John motioned and said, "All right, Barney, get in."

Barney ran around and made a leap, landing in the back of the truck. He moved up behind the cab and sat down. He had learned that the cab was a good wind break.

Well, Doc Miller put twenty-one stitches in Amber's leg. They were very evenly spaced—a work of art. And true to her promise, Amber never went near ole Satan again.

Chapter Five

The Grizzly

One rainy morning, in early spring, Barney was out making his rounds. As he was cutting through the maternity pasture, he came upon a dead, half-eaten baby calf.

Dixie, the calf's mother, was all upset and, of course, would not let Barney near her baby. She knew he hadn't done this terrible thing to her baby. She knew for a fact who had done it.

Barney sniffed the ground, then asked, "Dixie, did a bear do this? I saw a grizzly yesterday."

Dixie mooed a soft moo and nosed her newborn baby. She said, "It was a huge bear, Barney, and it was mean!" Then, lowering her head, she asked, "Why did it have to kill my baby?"

Barney said, "Grizzlies are just naturally mean. Don't worry, Dixie, I'll fix that bear! I'll fix him good! I'll make sure he never messes with this farm again!"

Well, while Barney was sniffing the dead baby calf, trying to pick up the bear's scent, Farmer John walked up.

Now, when Farmer John saw Barney standing over the dead baby calf, with a little blood on his nose, he came to the wrong conclusion. He took off his hat and scratched his head, then asked a terrible thing. With disgust in his eyes and a frown on his face, he asked, "Barney, why did you kill that calf?"

Barney's tail drooped, and he lowered his head, surprised at the terrible question. He thought, "I've guarded this place faithfully, and this is the thanks I get."

"Go, Barney! Git on home! I'll deal with you later!" Farmer John said with a scowl. "I can't believe you'd do something like this."

Barney turned and, with his head hung low, headed for the house. When he glanced back, Farmer John was standing there, watching him. He took a shortcut through the woods. He ran with his nose to the ground, following the grizzly's trail.

Trotting through the woods, he thought, "I'll show him. I'll show 'em all. I'll track down that grizzly! I don't want Farmer John or anyone else thinking that I killed that calf."

When he got to the barn, he crawled under the side shed that was connected to it and lay there waiting for his master—waiting for the whipping that was sure to come—the whipping he did not deserve.

Barney was lying there thinking about the grizzly, dozing off, just about asleep, when he heard a distant roar. At first, he thought he was dreaming, so he didn't do more than open one eye and scan the pasture off to his left, then off to his right. When he saw nothing unusual, he closed that eye and dozed off again.

Suddenly, Barney sat straight up! The black hair on his back bristled. Every nerve in his body tingled, and every muscle in his body quivered. Barney knew somehow that the ole grizzly bear was near. Then—a roar! It came from the field that held the mama cows and their newborn babies. Barney "gave tongue" and took off!

Farmer John had just stepped off the back porch. He had decided that it was time to have that talk with Barney and was on his way to the side shed that was connected to the barn. He and Barney had heard the roar at the same time, but he wasn't sure which direction it had come from.

When Barney took off toward the east, Farmer John ran back inside and grabbed his rifle, loading it as he ran. He was right behind Barney, and they were running fast!

Barney knew by the sound of the bear's growl that it was after one of the animals. It was a furious growl, a killer growl! And Barney knew that. His legs were flying and his heart

was racing! Then he heard the angry
bawl of a mother cow and thought,
"That bear's after one of the babies!"

Farmer John knew now that the commotion was coming from the maternity ward, as he called it. He remembered that Bossy had calved that morning. He and Barney had watched from the lane when they were checking the cows.

He checked his gun, making sure he had loaded it with real bullets and not rock salt. He kept rock salt in one pocket of his overalls and shells in the other. He used the rock salt for shoot-ing pesky animals in the behind so they would leave his garden, his cows, and his baby calves alone. The rock salt would sting the ole bear, and it would make it madder and meaner than ever! This time, he had real bullets in his gun.

Bossy bawled again, and, again, Barney picked up speed. When he reached the fence that encircled the maternity ward, he didn't stop and crawl under—he sailed up and over!

While Barney was still in mid-air, he caught a glimpse of something golden brown. When he got closer, he saw the dreaded creature who was after Bossy's new baby. It was a huge brown grizzly!

When the bear saw Barney, it stood on its back legs and let out a roar! Bossy was between her calf and the grizzly, desperately trying to save her baby.

The bear had holes in his chest where Bossy had pierced him with her horns. Bossy had slashes across her shoulder and neck where the bear had slashed her with his claws.

Barney knew when he saw Bossy that she had fought a fierce

fight, but now she was beginning to weaken. Her legs were wobbly.

Barney circled the bear. Every nerve in his body tingled, and the hair on his neck and back stood up.

The bear's eyes were on Barney, but he was distracted when the little baby calf let out a cry. He seemed to forget about Barney. He whirled and started for the calf.

When Bossy saw the grizzly heading for her baby again, she did the natural thing; she lowered her head and charged!

The bear had just reached the calf when Bossy's horns hooked him in the side! He stumbled sideways, surprised by her sudden attack.

Barney knew that the bear could kill Bossy with just one powerful blow of his mighty paw. He knew the baby calf would be a goner, too, if he didn't do something fast!

Now, the bear was really mad! He let out a loud, angry roar.

Bossy was mad, too! She was slinging her head from side to side and frothing at the mouth. And of course, the baby calf was terrified! It was a girl—a little heifer.

The little heifer's heart was pounding, and she was crying. She knew something was very wrong. And of course, she sensed the danger associated with the smell of the wild animal.

The grizzly was standing on his back legs, towering above the little heifer. Just as the grizzly dropped to the ground and reached for her, Barney made a lunge! He landed on the grizzly's back and sank his teeth into the side of its neck. The bear slung his head from side to side, but Barney held on tight.

All the animals in the edge of the woods were watching the fierce struggle. And of course, they were rooting for Barney. They didn't want that grizzly around. He was nothing but trouble.

Barney had a strong hold on the bear's neck. His jaws were locked tight.

Barney knew now that he had no choice; he would have to kill the bear, or it would kill the baby calf—and maybe himself and Bossy, too. There was no turning back.

Farmer John had just crawled through the fence. His chest was heaving; he was out of breath. He stopped and threw up his gun, taking aim at the bear.

Barney had a good grip on the bear. His sharp teeth had pierced a vein. He could taste blood.

Just then, Farmer John yelled, "Barney! Turn loose! Get back so I can shoot that dad-blamed grizzly!"

Barney heard Farmer John's voice, and it startled him. His grip loosened a little. He knew by the tone of his master's voice that he had been told to do something. He had always minded Farmer John. He had always done what he was told to do, but what now?

He thought, "I just can't let go! I have to hold on! I can't let this bear kill Bossy's calf!"

The grizzly had felt Barney's hold loosen, and he reached back and pulled him from his neck. He threw him about six feet away, and Barney landed with a thump and a bounce.

The grizzly's eyes were on the newborn calf. He let out an angry growl that seemed to grow as he opened his mouth.

Even though the breath had been knocked from him when he landed on the ground, Barney made another lunge for the bear!

The bear had just reached the baby calf and was about to make the kill when Barney hit him. Again, he went for the throat. He instinctively sank his teeth into the very spot he had already torn open.

Ole Barney must have weighed eighty pounds—only one-eighth the weight of the bear. Even though the bear weighed eight times as much, he was no match for Barney, because Barney was protecting the place he loved. And, he was protecting his honor—his good name. After all, hadn't Farmer John accused him of killing the first calf? That accusation had hurt him; it had hurt him a lot!

What followed then is hard to describe. Things happened so fast! At one point the bear tore Barney loose, and then, with a mighty swipe, sliced open Barney's side. The bear's sharp claws caught Barney on his left side, at his front shoulder, and went all the way to his hip.

Barney felt pain! His side hurt! It stung! It burned! And the pain did one more thing; it made him mad!

Barney was on his feet again— his hair bristling. It was easy to see that he was ready to tear the grizzly's head off!

Suddenly, Bossy stopped bellowing. The baby calf stopped crying. Farmer John stopped yelling. Even the animals in the edge of the woods held their breath. There was total silence. Everyone's eyes were on Barney.

Barney was standing there glaring at the bear. Then, he let out a long, deep howl. It was a howl that Roy Raccoon recognized. It was a howl that little Chrissy Cottontail recognized. It was a howl that Sammy Skunk recognized. It was a howl that all the animals that were gathered in the edge of the woods recognized. It was Barney's "gotcha" howl. And they all knew what it meant.

Barney's muscles tightened, and he assumed a crouch. He barred his sharp teeth and, with blood spurting from the four wounds in his side and a growl coming from deep in his throat, he lunged at the grizzly!

Long sharp teeth grabbed the grizzly's throat. They went round and around.

Suddenly, Barney let go and dropped to the ground. He took off toward the bluff that overlooked the river. When he was about ten feet away, he stopped and looked back. The bear was right behind him.

Barney growled, showing his teeth, and the growl made the grizzly even madder. With his long sharp claws, he made a swipe at Barney, but Barney ducked and swerved to the right.

It was now apparent to Barney that his plan would work. All he had to do was outsmart the grizzly.

Barney made a wide circle around the bear, then, with his body close to the ground, darted in and nipped the back of its leg. The bear whirled and let out an angry roar!

Barney made another pass. He circled, nipped, and retreated over and over again.

The grizzly bear grew madder and madder! All the time, Barney kept luring it to the edge of the cliff. Again he gave out his "gotcha" howl. He circled, and this time, took a hunk out of the grizzly's leg. It screamed like a panther! Then, with glowing red eyes, it lunged for Barney.

Barney was in position. He had stopped at the very edge of the cliff.

When the grizzly lunged, Barney stepped to the side, and the bear went over the edge.

The grizzly fell, with a thud, to the riverbank below.

Barney ran to the edge and looked over. The grizzly was lying there, with its head at an odd angle. Barney hurried down the bank and, placing his front feet on the grizzly's head, let out a low warning growl.

In the distance, thunder rumbled, and lightning danced across the sky. A storm was brewing. No one moved. Not a sound could be heard but the distant thunder.

During the fierce struggle, the animals in the edge of the woods had not moved a muscle. Now, they crept closer to get a better view.

The milk cows in the nearby

fields had gathered near the fence. They had stood, motionless, with their eyes glued on Barney and the bear. They now pushed against the fence, craning their necks, trying to see.

For the last five minutes or so, Farmer John had watched Barney, with a proud look on his face. He had realized early on what Barney was up to. He lowered his gun and quickly checked Bossy and her calf.

After he was satisfied that Bossy and her baby were okay, Farmer John made his way down the side of the cliff to the bank of the river. When he reached the bear and ole Barney, he stopped and raised his gun, taking aim.

The grizzly bear didn't move. Farmer John poked it with his gun, but the bear didn't move a muscle. The fall had broken its neck.

After waiting for a couple of seconds, Farmer John pushed back his hat, looked at Barney, and said, "I think you've killed this dad-blamed grizzly! Yes sireee, Barney, I think you've killed yourself a bear!"

Barney heard Farmer John's voice, but he couldn't respond. He had collapsed and couldn't get up. He just didn't have the strength. Blood was still flowing from the deep wounds in his side. He was slowly bleeding to death.

Chapter Six

Catgut and a Needle

The animals watched closely as Farmer John gently picked up Barney and headed for the house. They eased over to the bear and sniffed it, and the smell made them shiver.

When Farmer John reached the fence he had crawled through earlier, he laid Barney on the ground. Once he was through the fence, he got down on his knees, reached out, and gently pulled Barney under.

Farmer John stopped several times before he reached the house, because Barney was heavy—dead weight.

When he neared the barn, he stopped and said, "Maybe I'd better put Barney in here. I don't want the girls to see him; at least, not yet, and they'll be home from school soon."

There was some loose straw in the corner, on the north side of the barn, and that's where Farmer John laid ole Barney. He gave Barney a reassuring pat on the head, then ran to the house, yelling, "Molly! I need your help!"

Molly was behind the house hanging clothes on the line. She had spent more time than usual performing the task because she had been listening to the terrible commotion that had been going on down in the field. When she heard Farmer John calling, she hurried to meet him.

She asked, "John, what in the world was going on down in the maternity pasture? Was that a bear I heard?"

"Yeah, Molly, it was," Farmer John answered. "It was a big ole grizzly bear. It was the biggest dad-blamed grizzly I've ever seen! It must have been that grizzly who killed that calf, and not ole Barney, like I'd thought."

"I heard Barney let out a howl. Did he chase the grizzly off?" she asked.

"You could say that, I reckon," Farmer John answered, with a grin. Then he added, "Ole Barney killed the grizzly, Molly. He killed that dad-blamed bear!"

Molly's mouth flew open. She stared at Farmer John, then asked, "And Barney? Did that bear kill Barney, John?"

Farmer John shook his head. Then, as if suddenly remembering, he turned and ran into the house, with Molly close behind.

He said, "No, but hurry, Molly! He's hurt bad! I carried him home. He's out in the barn lying in the straw. Let's find a disinfectant and something to bandage him up with."

As Molly grabbed a handful of swabs, she said, "Get an old sheet, John. We'll tear it into long strips for bandages."

Farmer John searched until he found an old sheet, then he hurried to the kitchen. He pulled out two or three drawers, then asked, "Molly, where are the dad-blamed scissors?"

Molly went to the drawers on the left of the sink and pulled out the second drawer down. She grabbed the scissors and made seven cuts across the entire length of the sheet. She handed the sheet to Farmer John and said, "Finish tearing the strips, then bring them to the barn. I'm going on."

Molly hurried out the door and down the steps, then turned and yelled, "Now, don't get the strips dirty, John!"

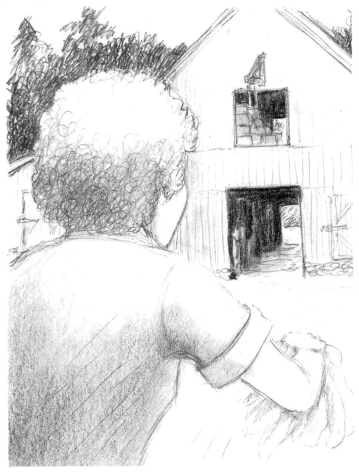

Farmer John and Molly, using the swabs and kerosene, cleaned Barney's wounds. And then, with experienced hands, Farmer John began sewing him up.

Barney felt the needle go in and out, in and out, all the way down his left side—four times. There were four long rows of stitches, and he felt every one of them.

Lying on the workbench in the barn, Barney slowly lifted his head and looked around.

Just then, Farmer John laid the needle and catgut down and said, "There now, Barney. That ought to do it. You'll soon be good as new."

Barney tried to sit up, but it hurt too much. A moan escaped his lips. Molly said, "Help him, John. He doesn't need to be straining himself. Pick him up easy-like and lay him on this quilt I brought from the house."

Barney watched as Molly placed the quilt on the ground in the corner of the barn. He cringed as Farmer John eased one hand under his neck and his other hand under his hips. A low whining sound escaped his lips as Farmer John lifted him and carried him over to the corner and laid him on the quilt.

As he stroked Barney's head, Farmer John said, "You're a good boy, Barney. You killed that mean ole grizzly, and you saved Bossy's calf. You just rest now. You'll be okay. Molly brought you a cool drink of water."

Barney's eyes followed Farmer John out the door. Then, he slowly closed his eyes and fell into a deep, troubled sleep. His eyes started twitching, and his legs started jerking. In his dream, he was fighting with the grizzly.

When the school bus stopped at the top of the hill, Barney's eyes slowly opened. He drifted in and out of sleep until he heard the little girls' voices. He listened as Farmer John related to them his terrible struggle with the grizzly.

Oohs and aahs and a couple of gasps came from the three girls. He heard Farmer John say, "Yes, sireee, ladies, from now on, our Barney will have a new name."

Barney's ears perked up as they asked, "What is it, Daddy? What's Barney's new name?"

Farmer John tipped back his hat, smiled a proud smile, and said, "Barney the Bear Killer!"